I WISH I HAD A DINOSAUR

IAN ANGGABRATA with MINGGA ANGGAWAN illustrated by PETER SHEEHAN

SCHOLASTIC INC.

New York Toronto London Auckland Sydney
Mexico City New Delhi Hong Kong Buenos Aires

For Mum and Dad, and for Ivan who loves dinosaurs as much as I do.
—I.A.

Special thanks to Margrete Lamond.
—P.S.

ISBN 0-439-80380-2

Illustrations by Peter Sheehan

12 11 10 9 8 7 6 5 4 3 5 6 7 8 9 10/0

Printed in the U.S.A.
First printing, November 2005

I wish I had a dinosaur.

I could slide right down

from my balcony.

We wouldn't have to run

past the dog that lives next door.

She could take me to school
much faster than the bus.

We wouldn't need the bus for field trips.

We wouldn’t even need the monkey bars.

Well, we might not be invited to birthday parties.

Balloons are just not for dinosaurs.

We might not be allowed to play in the park.

Or sunbathe on the beach.

But I guess I could take her to the library.

Dinosaurs are not book eaters,
after all.

I would take her to my swimming class

so I could float without the kickboard.

My dinosaur could even take us to the zoo.

My dinosaur could help Dad
prune the trees.

And clean the backyard.

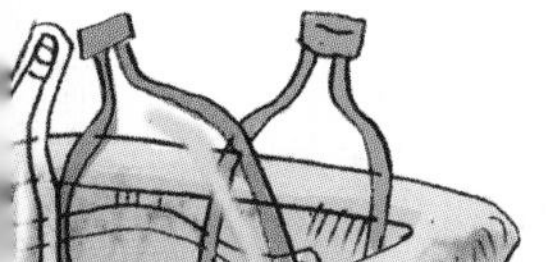

Or she could go to the supermarket with Mom

and help with her shopping.

She could help me finish my dinner.

Then I would watch the sunset

from the highest hammock of all.

And of course I wouldn't need Mom to sit with me at night, with my dinosaur sleeping by my side.